CAROLINE PITCHER took her degree in English and
European Literature at Warwick University and later became
a primary school teacher in East London. Her other books for Frances Lincoln
include *Lord of the Forest*, *The Time of the Lion* and *Mariana and the Merchild*
(all illustrated by Jackie Morris), and *The Winter Dragon* and *Nico's Octopus*.
Caroline lives in Derby.

JACKIE MORRIS wanted to be an artist from the age of six.
At school she got into trouble for drawing and dreaming –
and now she says she gets paid for both! Her much-admired books
include *Lord of the Forest*, *Mariana and the Merchild*,
The Time of the Lion and *The Snow Whale*, all with Caroline Pitcher,
and *Can You See A Little Bear?* with James Mayhew,
which was chosen as Best Book of the Year 2005 by Child Magazine, USA.
Jackie has also collaborated with Mary Hoffman on
Parables, *Miracles* and *Animals of the Bible*, and with
Sally Lloyd-Jones on *Little One, We Knew You'd Come*.
She herself has written and illustrated *The Seal Children*.
Jackie lives in Pembrokeshire.

For Wendy – C.P.

For Hannah Lily Sunshine, with love – J.M.

The Snow Whale copyright © Frances Lincoln Limited 1996
Text copyright © Caroline Pitcher 1996
Illustrations copyright © Jackie Morris 1996

First published in Great Britain in 1996 by Frances Lincoln Children's Books,
74-77 White Lion Street London N1 9PF
www.franceslincoln.com

This edition published in Great Britain in 2008

British Library Cataloguing in Publication Data available on request

ISBN: 978-1-84507-717-4

Printed in China

3 5 7 9 8 6 4 2

The Snow Whale

Caroline Pitcher

Illustrated by
Jackie Morris

F

FRANCES LINCOLN
CHILDREN'S BOOKS

One November night, snow fell fast and thick as down from a duck's back.
In the morning, the hills were hump-backed with snow.

Laurie ran into the garden and searched for a stick.
She drew a great shape in the hillside.
Her little brother Leo ploughed through the snow after her,
holding high his bucket and spade.

"What shall I do?" he asked.
"Pile up the snow," she said.

"What are you building?"
"A whale."

"Where does the snow come from?" asked Leo.
His sister sighed. "Don't you know *anything*?" she said.
"The water rises up from the sea and goes into
the clouds. Sometimes it comes down again as snow."

Out ran Rory from next door. He brought his wheelbarrow to help, and his sister Kate brought a garden rake.

"Where will the whale swim?" asked Leo.

Nobody answered. They were too busy huffing and puffing, bringing the whale out of the hill.

"Fetch me the rake, Leo," said Laurie.

"Why?"

"To draw his tail flukes and his big filter mouth."

"But what will he eat?" asked Leo.

Nobody answered, so he brought her the rake.

"Fetch me Dad's ladder, Leo,"
said Laurie.
"Why?"
"To climb up his back
and make his blow-hole."
"What will he blow?" asked Leo.
Nobody answered, so he
brought her the ladder.
On the way back, he found
a special stone on the path.

"Here's the whale's eye!" he cried.
"It's very tiny," said Laurie.
"But it looks happy," said Leo,
and he climbed up to put it
on the whale's face.

They shovelled and dug and bucketed and wheeled
and packed and patted and polished and smoothed.
Then they stood back and looked.

He was the most beautiful snow whale in the whole world:
high as a church, round as a cloud, white as an ice-floe.

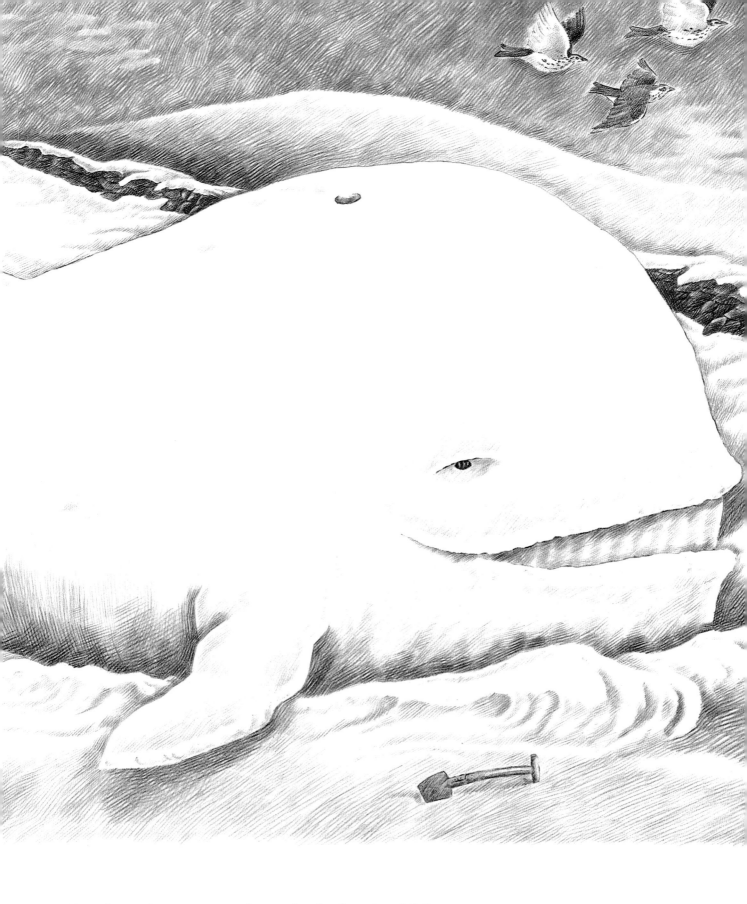

In the afternoon the whale looked blue.

"That's because he's freezing," said Laurie, "and so am I."

They ran home to thaw their fingers and dry their gloves
and socks, and to eat hot toast and cake.

As darkness settled over the hillside, Laurie and Leo
watched the whale from their window.
"The valley is just a jam-jar to him," said Laurie. "If he sang,
his voice would shatter the hills. If he thrashed his tail,
he would break our house in two."

Next day it was so cold that the snow whale's mouth was full of icicles. The children played with him all day. They ran round him, climbed on his back and slid down his sides.

They sailed him over the seven seas. They told him
stories about ants and elephants and made him smile.

Later, when the sun broke through and water-drops dripped from the branches, the snow whale glistened like silver.
"Where does the snow go?" asked Leo.
His sister sighed.
"Don't you know *anything*?" she said.
"It melts and flows back into the rivers and down into the seas again."

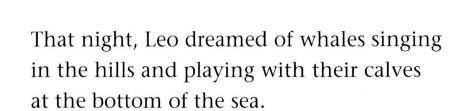

That night, Leo dreamed of whales singing
in the hills and playing with their calves
at the bottom of the sea.

When he woke, someone was crying, but it wasn't
the whale. It was Laurie.
"Where has the whale gone?" she sobbed.
"I *do* know that," Leo said, and put his arms round her.
"He's gone back to the sea again. Snow Whale's gone home."

MORE FRANCES LINCOLN TITLES FROM CAROLINE PITCHER AND JACKIE MORRIS

Lord of the Forest

For Little Tiger, every sound he hears in the forest is exciting and new.
But each time he tells his mother, she replies, "When you don't hear them,
my son, be ready. *The Lord of the Forest* is here!" Tiger is puzzled and asks
his friends – strutting Peacock, blundering Rhino and trumpeting Elephant –
to help him decide: who is the Lord of the Forest?

ISBN 978-1-84507-276-6

Mariana and the Merchild

Old Mariana longs for friendship, but she is feared by the village
children and fearful of the hungry sea-wolves hiding in the caves
near her hut. Then one day she finds a Merbaby inside a crab shell and
at once she loves it more than life itself – although she knows that one day,
when the sea is calm again, the Merchild's mother will come
to take her daughter back again.

ISBN 978-1-84507-708-2

The Time of the Lion

At night, while his village sleeps, Joseph hears a lion's roar thunderclap
across the wide East African Savannah. When he sees the lion racing
towards him, his great head streaming with gold, a special friendship begins,
and every noon-time Joseph visits the lion's grassy den to talk, meet
his lioness and watch the cubs at play. But one day traders come
looking for lion cubs, and Joseph suspects that his father
has betrayed his newfound friends …

ISBN 978-0-7112-1338-8